TEN LiTTLE ROBOTS

MIKE BROWNLOW SIMON RICKERTY

Ten little robots, gleaming, sparkly new.
Power on, lights blink – they wonder what to do.

"This factory looks exciting. Shall we take a peep?"
Ten little robots all say,

"BEEEP!"

WARNING DANGER!

Ten little robots miss a warning sign.

"NEEE NAA

10

nine

Nine little robots

stumble through a gate.

9

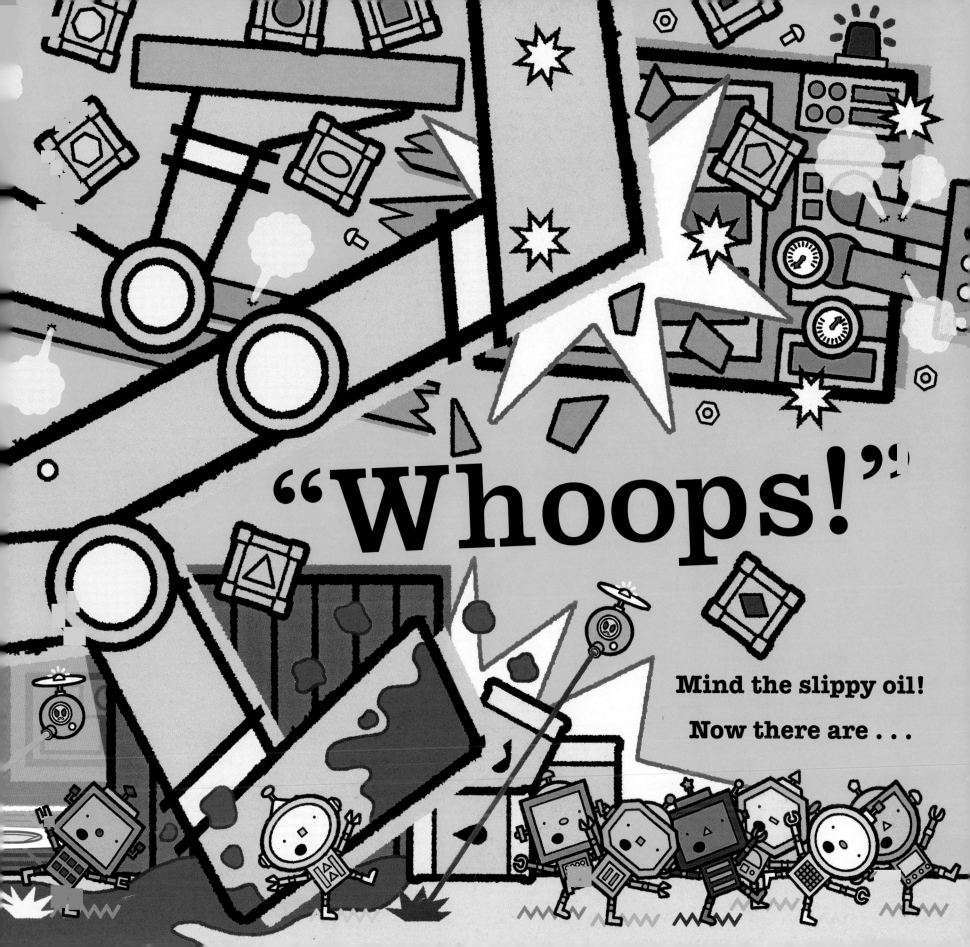

"Whoops!"

Mind the slippy oil!

Now there are . . .

...eight.

Eight little robots – it's hot just like an oven.

8

"KERBOOOOM!"

goes the engine room.

Now there are . . .

seven

Seven little robots

dodge the crashing bricks.

7

CHOOO CHO

OO! goes the tiny train. Now there are . . .

6 . . . **six.**

Six little robots running for their lives.

T H U M P !

go the

crusher's

hammers.

Now there are . . .

. . . **five.**

Five little robots fear the
furnace roar.

5

...four.

Four little robots
trying to wriggle free.

4

. . . three.

Three little robots
above the
molten brew.

CRACKLE! FIZZLE! go the sparks.

Now there are . . .

. . . **two.**

Two little robots

duck the laser gun.

2

One little robot, dangling from a rope.

Can he save the others?

Mustn't give up hope!

Fighting through the wreckage,
climbing through the mess.

Plug the holes.

Fix the pipes.

Can he mend it?

YES!

Hooray! The danger's over!

Their buzzers chirp and cheep!

Ten little robots all shout,

"BEEEEP!"

For Rex
M.B.

For E-BOT and I-BOT
S.R.

ORCHARD BOOKS

First published in Great Britain in 2018 by The Watts Publishing Group
This edition first published in 2018

1 3 5 7 9 10 8 6 4 2

Text © Mike Brownlow, 2018
Illustrations © Simon Rickerty, 2018

HB ISBN 978 1 40833 823 0
PB ISBN 978 1 40833 824 7

Printed and bound in China

Orchard Books
An imprint of Hachette Children's Group
Part of The Watts Publishing Group Limited
Carmelite House
50 Victoria Embankment
London EC4Y 0DZ

An Hachette UK Company
www.hachette.co.uk

www.hachettechildrens.co.uk